DUDLEY'S TEA PARTY

WRITTEN BY ALEX GALATIS
ILLUSTRATED BY JOSEPH SHERMAN

SCHOLASTIC INC.

New York   Toronto   London   Auckland   Sydney

ISBN 0-590-47494-4

Book designed by Nancy Levin Kipnis

12 11 10 9 8 7 6 5 4 3 2   5 6 7 8 9/9 0/0

Printed in the U.S.A.   24

First Scholastic printing, August 1995

Dudley the Dragon just loved to wash and splash and play in the bathtub. He loved to watch the bubbles tumble over the top of the tub in a giant wave.

"Dudley!" Sally yelled from the kitchen. "What are you doing in there?"

"Nothing!" Dudley yelled back. "Just having a bath."

3

"The Robins are going to be here any minute," said Sally. "You invited them over for tea."

"Splash you," said Dudley.

"You wouldn't dare," said Sally.

Ker-splash! Dudley splashed Sally with a big wave of sudsy water.

"Now the water's too cold. It needs more hot," Dudley said. But when Dudley went to turn on the water, the faucet came off in his hand. Water gushed out all over the bathroom.

4

Meanwhile, Charles and Tiffany Robin were in the living room waiting for their tea. There was nothing the Robins liked more than a delicious cup of dragonberry tea. Sally entered from the bathroom covered with bubbles.

"Where's all that water coming from?" asked Mr. Robin.

"It's coming from the bathtub" Matt explained as he ran to the bathroom.

"I'll get you some tea," said Sally. She went into the kitchen.

Just as Sally put the teabag in the teapot, Matt and Dudley slid into the kitchen, very wet and covered with soapy bubbles. Sally turned on the faucet.

"That's strange," said Sally. "There's no water in the kitchen."

"A mystery!" said Matt.

In fact, there was no more water anywhere in Dudley's house. Even his bathtub had run dry.

Matt turned on the television in the kitchen to find out why there was no more water. The woman on TV said there was a water shortage.

"What does that mean?" asked Dudley.

"It means too much water was being used in wasteful ways by someone silly," said the woman on TV. "Now, who could that have been?"

Matt and Sally looked at Dudley.

7

"But I need water," said Dudley. "I promised the Robins a cup of tea."

"Then we'll find some," said Matt. "Now, where do we get water from?"

"The sky," said Dudley.

They all looked up but there wasn't a rain cloud in the sky.

"How about a pond?" said Sally.

"Yes, there's lots of water there," said Dudley. "We'll just go down and borrow a teapot of water from Sammy the Frog."

The Robins were
still sitting in the living room
waiting for their tea.

"There are sandwiches in the kitchen," said Sally as she ran out the door.

"Help yourself," said Matt, following Sally.

"We won't be long," said Dudley as he left the cave.

"I sure would like a cup of tea," said Mrs. Robin.

Matt, Sally, and Dudley rushed over to the pond where Sammy the Frog was having fun playing his saxophone.

"Hey, it's my big green buddy," Sammy said. "What can I do for you?"

"I was wondering if I might please borrow a teapot of water?" asked Dudley.

"Help yourself, dragon," said Sammy. "But I'm not sure this is the right kind of water for tea."

"Yuck!" said Dudley. "Not unless you like your tea extra muddy."

Splat! Dudley spilled the muddy water from his teapot.

"This isn't water for people to drink," said Sammy. "It's water for frogs to live in."

"Now what do we do?" asked Dudley.

"Think like a detective. Now where is there water?" Matt wondered. "I've got it. I know where there's a lot of water. Follow me."

Back in Dudley's living room, the Robins were getting very thirsty.

"It's taking Mr. Dudley a long time to make our tea," said Mr. Robin.

"A very long time. I wonder where he is?" asked Mrs. Robin.

12

"The ocean," said Matt, pointing at the waves. "Didn't I tell you this was a good idea? More water than you could ever use."

"It sure is big," said Dudley.

"But you can't drink this!" said Sally. "It's seawater. It's too salty. Try it."

"Yuck!
This is awful!"
said Dudley.
"There's so much water
and we can't drink it! That's not fair," said Matt.
Dudley felt bad. He thought about how much water
he had wasted. Maybe there would be water for tea if he
hadn't let the tap run when he was brushing his teeth.

6

Just then water poured down from the sky, soaking Dudley, Matt, and Sally. But there wasn't a rain cloud to be seen. How could that be?

"Look! Out in the ocean," said Sally, pulling a telescope out of her bag. "It's a whale!"

"Ahoy there!" said the whale. "My name is Katrina. I'm the quickest, slickest whale this side of the ocean blue."

"My name is Dudley. You know, you don't see many whales where I live."

"Well, you don't see many dragons where I live," said Katrina.

"Hey, why don't I show you where I live? I heard you talking about water. No one knows more about water than Katrina the Whale."

"Sounds like fun," said Sally. "Let's go."

Meanwhile,
back in Dudley's
cave, the Robins were waiting
for their tea.
"I'm sure they'll be back any minute now
with our tea," said Mrs. Robin. "I mean, how far
could they have gone?"

17

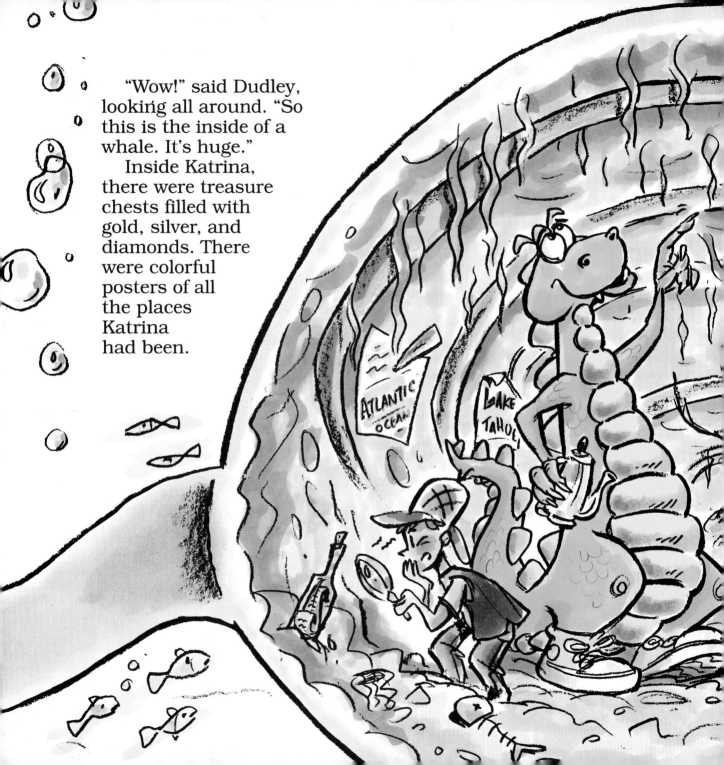

"Wow!" said Dudley, looking all around. "So this is the inside of a whale. It's huge."

Inside Katrina, there were treasure chests filled with gold, silver, and diamonds. There were colorful posters of all the places Katrina had been.

There were boats, seaweed, ship anchors, and lots of water.

"So much water," sighed Dudley. "So little tea."

"Look! You can even see her ribs," said Sally.

"Let's look around and see what else we can see," said Matt.

Through the underwater windows, Dudley, Matt, and Sally could see the wonders of the ocean.

"I've never seen anything like this before," said Dudley, pointing to an octopus. "There are so many different kinds of fish. Big fish. Little fish. Fish of all colors. They're beautiful."

Matt and Sally could see sea horses galloping, starfish twinkling, and little baby fishes swimming to school.

"I guess we're not the only ones who need water," said Sally.

"Every living thing needs water," Matt agreed.

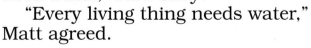

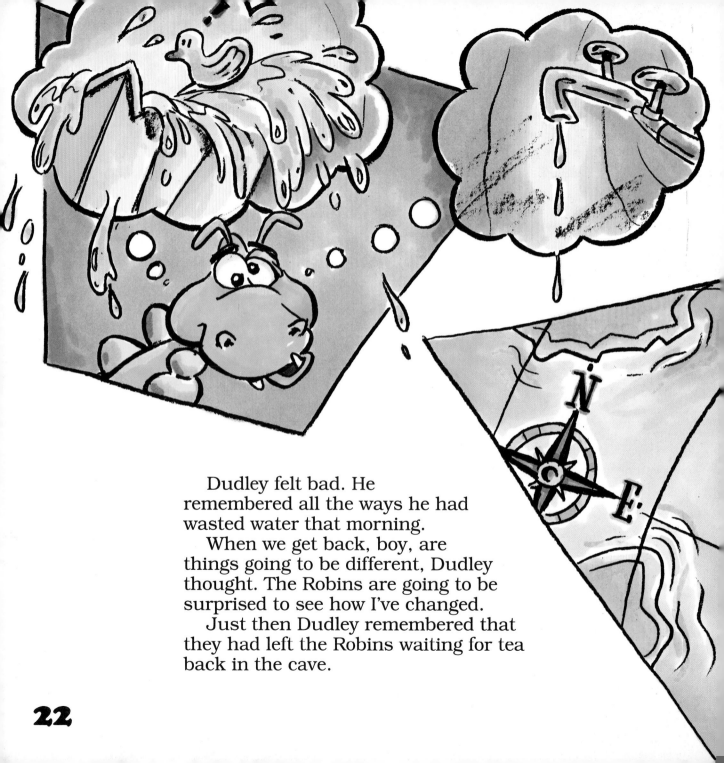

Dudley felt bad. He remembered all the ways he had wasted water that morning.

When we get back, boy, are things going to be different, Dudley thought. The Robins are going to be surprised to see how I've changed.

Just then Dudley remembered that they had left the Robins waiting for tea back in the cave.

"Katrina! We have to get back home right away," said Dudley. "Could you help us out?"

So Katrina, the quickest, slickest whale in all the ocean, swam as fast as she could.

"Hold on tight, everyone!" said Katrina as she swam faster than she had ever swum before.

"Thank
you for the ride,"
Sally said with a wave.
"Bye-bye," said Katrina. She
jumped high in the air and then . . .*Splash!*
. . . dived deep into the ocean.
"We have to hurry back to the Robins," said Dudley.
"But we still don't have any water for the tea," said Matt.
"Then we'll drink something else," Dudley answered. "Do
the Robins drink lemonade?"

"Dudley, lemonade has water in it, too," said Sally.

"This is more serious than I thought," Dudley said.

In Dudley's living room, the Robins were so tired of waiting for their tea, they fell asleep.

"Zzzzz," said Mr. Robin.

"Zzzzz," said Mrs. Robin. Under her breath she whispered the word, " . . . tea . . . "

    Just then
the sky got very dark.
Black clouds clustered together.
Sally looked up and pulled out an umbrella
from her bag.
    "Now where are we going to find water?"
Matt asked.
    "I don't know," said Dudley.
    Sally smiled. She knew what was about
to happen.

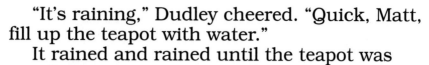

"It's raining," Dudley cheered. "Quick, Matt, fill up the teapot with water."

It rained and rained until the teapot was overflowing.

"Now, let's get home quickly and make the Robins a big pot of tea," said Dudley.

27

"It's nice to be home again," said Dudley as he poured the hot water into the teapot. "These tiny sandwiches will be perfect for the Robins to eat with my special dragonberry tea."

Matt
and Sally dried
themselves with towels. It was
nice to finally be home, warm and dry.

Matt looked at the kitchen tap. It was dripping.

"That means the water is back on again," said
Matt. "You mean, we went on that search for
nothing?"

"Not for nothing," said Dudley. "I learned a lot
about how important it is not to waste water."

"Wait a minute," said Sally. "If the kitchen tap
is dripping that means . . ."

They all stopped and thought about the same
thing at the same time.

"The bathroom!!!"

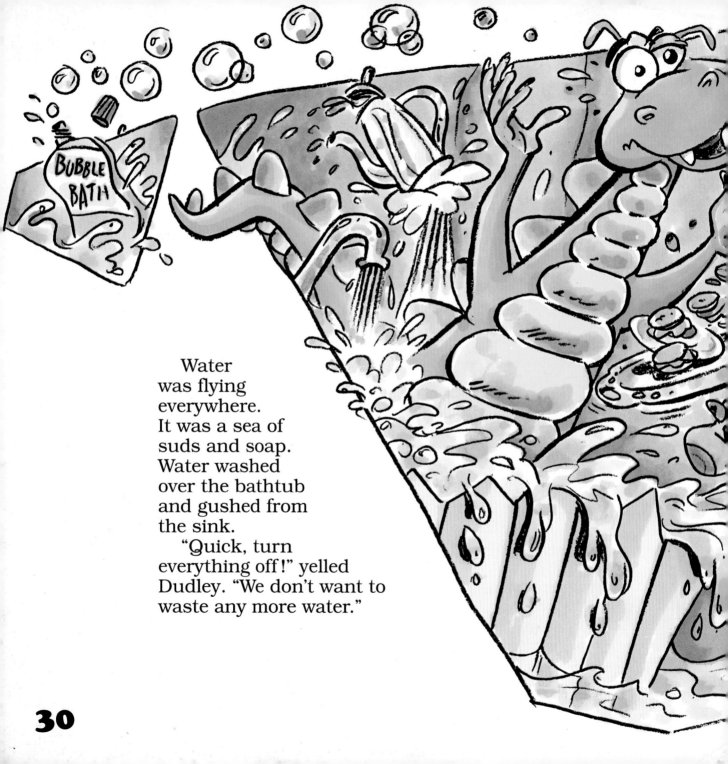

Water
was flying
everywhere.
It was a sea of
suds and soap.
Water washed
over the bathtub
and gushed from
the sink.

"Quick, turn
everything off!" yelled
Dudley. "We don't want to
waste any more water."

Back in Dudley's living room, the Robins were about to leave.

"Let's go home, Tiffany," said Mr. Robin. "I'll make you a nice pot of tea back at the nest."

"Good idea, Charles," said Mrs. Robin. "I don't think we'll ever get a cup of tea here."

Finally, Dudley, Matt, and Sally turned off all the water and entered the living room wet and covered with suds.

"Where are the Robins?" asked Sally.

Dudley looked all around.

"That's funny. They left without their tea!" Dudley said. "Well, how do you like that!"